KNIGHTS

vs.

THE END

(OF *EVERYTHING*)

MATT PHELAN

KNIGHTS
vs.
THE END
(OF *EVERYTHING*)

GREENWILLOW BOOKS
An Imprint of HarperCollinsPublishers

The text of this book is set in Iowan Old Style. Book design by Sylvie Le Floc'h

Library of Congress Cataloging-in-Publication Data: Names: Phelan, Matt, author, illustrator.
Title: Knights vs. the end (of everything) / written and illustrated by Matt Phelan. Other
    titles: Knights versus the end (of everything)
Description: First edition. | New York, NY : Greenwillow Books, an Imprint of HarperCollins
    Publishers, [2020] | Audience: Ages 8–12 | Audience: Grades 4–6 | Summary: "The four daring
    knights and one intrepid archer enter the Faerie Realm, where they find dangerous warlocks,
    a mysterious knight, and one very nasty dragon"—Provided by publisher.
Identifiers: LCCN 2019041787 | ISBN 9780062910974 (hardcover)
Subjects: CYAC: Knights and knighthood—Fiction. | Characters in Literature—Fiction.
    | Adventure and adventurers—Fiction. | Fantasy. | Humorous stories.
Classification: LCC PZ7.P44882 Knq 2020 | DDC [Fic]—dc23 LC record available at https://
    lccn.loc.gov/2019041787

20 21 22 23 24 PC/LSCH 10 9 8 7 6 5 4 3 2 1 First Edition   Greenwillow Books

FOR JASPER AND NORA

CONTENTS

CHAPTER ONE

SIR GAWAIN & THE GREEN KNIGHT (AND ALSO EREC)

On the last night of the year, a snowstorm engulfed Camelot. Outside the castle, the wind howled, the snow swirled, and the temperature dropped well below freezing.

Inside the castle, the thick stone walls, majestic tapestries, and blazing fires kept out the chill. The brave, good knights of King Arthur's court reveled in the cozy atmosphere, telling stories and jokes, singing songs and toasting good cheer.

Until . . .

The great oak doors burst open.

An enormous steed entered the main hall. It was twice the size of a normal horse. Stranger still was its color. It was completely green.

Riding the horse was a giant of a man—regal, strong, and every bit as green as his steed. Silence filled the hall.

The Green Knight dismounted. He held the finest, greenest battle-axe anyone had ever seen.

"Knights of the Round Table," bellowed the Green Knight, "I challenge one of you to take my mighty axe and deal me your finest blow. I shall not defend myself. Use all of your strength, and strike me well and true. Who is brave enough to accept?"

Sir Gawain, noblest of all, rose and stood before the Green Knight. Murmurs peppered the Round Table.

"One more thing," said the Green Knight. "If I survive your blow, in one year's time you must journey to my castle, where I will have *my* turn. I shall strike you with all of *my* might."

Gawain remained silent. Calm. Cool.

"Strike well, brave Gawain." The Green Knight offered his axe, a hint of a smile visible beneath his massive green beard.

Gawain took the axe.

"HOLD IT!" yelled a voice from outside the hall.

Sir Erec strode through the doors, past the green stallion, and right up to the standoff.

"I'll handle this," Erec said casually.

"I say, Erec," said Gawain.

In a flash, Erec took the axe, swung it wide, and sliced the Green Knight's head clean off. The head dropped to the stone floor with a thud. The body remained standing.

A collective gasp sounded from the Round Table.

Erec stepped toward the head.

"Up to your old tricks again, eh?" he said.

Erec gave the head a strong kick.

Another gasp came from the crowd.

The head soared across the hall toward the

door, where Sir Bors caught it as he ambled in.

"Unnecessary roughness!" the Green Knight's head roared, his eyes popping open. "Oh, for pity's sake. It's you."

"Hello, froggy!" said Bors with a grin.

"Bors!" grumbled the head. "Release me at once, you rotted stump."

"Gladly." Bors tossed the head over his shoulder. Sir Hector nimbly caught it as he strolled in.

"Tsk, tsk," said Hector. "What *are* we going to do with you?"

King Arthur rose. "Sir Erec, please explain," he said.

"Yes, Sire," said Erec. "This big lug," he continued, patting the still-standing, headless body, "is a bit of a troublemaker. Nothing *we* can't handle, of course."

"I, too, could have handled him," said Gawain evenly.

"Quite possibly, Gawain," said Erec. "But we

just saved you the bother. The Green Knight is a fairly elaborate prankster. We have experience with him."

"Meddlers, the lot of you!" yelled the green head. "No sense of humor at all. I've never met a worse gang of—"

"Language, Sir Green Knight," said Hector as he turned and lobbed the head into the shadows. The Black Knight entered next, holding it.

"Lady Magdalena!" cried the head. "Present company, excluded, of course. How are you, my dear?"

"Never better," said Magdalena with a smile. "And you?"

"Not bad. I wouldn't mind having my body back."

"Not quite yet," said Erec.

He turned to Arthur.

"My king, we have traveled for the past year. We have fought and defeated many monsters and creatures of the night that Morgause released into the world."

"But . . . ," began Arthur.

"But," Erec continued, "no sign of Morgause herself. Or her son Mordred."

"My mother is very clever, very powerful, and very

determined," said Gawain. "Capturing her will not be easy."

"We do not underestimate your mother, Sir Gawain," said Magdalena, joining the others. "We have had too much experience with her for that."

"My brothers Agravaine and Gareth continue their search as well. They were due back in Camelot on the solstice," said Gawain. "But we've had no word from them."

"Perhaps they have found her!" said Hector brightly.

"Wait," said the Green Knight's head. "My mind wandered a bit there. Ha! Joke!"

Bors chuckled. "I get it!"

"But seriously," continued the Green Knight, focusing on Magdalena. "Who are you talking about?"

"Morgause."

"Oh! *I've* seen her. Calls herself the Queen of Air and Darkness or some such rubbish. Not a pleasant human, that one."

"Where did you see her?" demanded Erec.

"She was visiting her sister. Morgan Le Fay."

Everyone in the hall caught their breath.

Queen Guinevere broke the hush.

"Morgan Le Fay the sorceress?" she whispered.

"The very same, Your Highness," said the Green Knight. "She's practically half-fay nowadays. I suppose that's where she got the name, now that I think about it."

"Can you take us to them?" asked Erec.

"Yes. But you might not like what you find."

The fire crackled. Erec, Hector, Bors, and Magdalena exchanged looks. A year's worth of searching, adventure, horror, and strife were perhaps nearing an end.

"Ahem," coughed the head. "Do you think I could get my body back now?"

CHAPTER TWO

BETTER
THAN AN OWL

Melancholy Postlethwaite stood in Merlin's tower studying an enormous book of spells. Hundreds and hundreds of beautifully bound volumes lined shelves that spiraled up, up, up the tower walls.

Merlin sat on a stool, gazing out the window. Archimedes the owl perched nearby, looking straight ahead (and certainly *not* at Merlin).

Mel turned her attention from the book to a stone on the table in front of her. She stared at it. She furrowed her brow.

The stone wobbled . . . and lifted into the air. It floated for a moment before dropping.

The owl made a little clicking sound.

"You are coming along splendidly, Mel," said Merlin brightly.

"It doesn't feel so. Maybe a wand would help?"

"Much magic deals with nudging the flow of natural forces, and the wood of certain trees *is* a natural conduit for that," said Merlin. "But a wand is not necessary."

Mel sighed. She gazed at the magical artifacts scattered about, the mysterious potions, the strange plants, the many books and baffling charts.

"It is all so complicated," she said.

Merlin looked up and smiled.

"It only appears so. It is simplicity itself. All you really need is experience, a bit of imagination, and a problem to sink your teeth into, so to speak. Those are the ideal ingredients for magic."

The owl ruffled his feathers quite loudly and flew up the rafters.

"Oh, that's enough of you!" said Merlin. "Mel is doing very well. Better than many I've taught, present company included."

"Do you talk to your owl a lot?" Mel asked.

"He used to talk back, but we had a bit of a disagreement concerning *the tree*."

Archimedes swooped down to the worktable and knocked over a beaker of green liquid. On purpose.

"You've mentioned a tree before. That you need to watch out for a certain one. Why? What can a tree do to you?" asked Mel.

"It is not what the tree will do, Mel. The tree is a destination of sorts. For me."

"I don't understand," said Mel.

"I do not expect you to," said Merlin. "Wheels are always in motion. I have my enemies. Certain outcomes may come to pass."

"Destiny?"

"Possibilities. But with possibilities, there is always choice." Merlin rose, took out his wand, and made the green puddle vanish. He selected a book and started to read, effectively ending the conversation.

A quiet knock sounded on the door and it creaked open. Sir Hector poked his head in.

"Excuse me, Merlin. I was wondering if I could have a word with Mel. *Oh!*"

Hector stepped slowly into the tower, his eyes wide.

"So . . . many . . . books!" he whispered. "How wonderful!"

"You are welcome to sit and read whenever you like, good Sir Hector," said Merlin.

"How I wish I could. A long evening in a comfortable chair with a book." Hector sighed.

He strained to see the highest shelves, bumping into a wooden lectern. A great leather-bound volume lay closed upon it. Scratches ran across the gold leaf title: *The Terrible Lizards*.

Hector jumped back.

Merlin smiled mischievously. "Go ahead. Open it. A good book should be reread from time to time."

"Most good books do not try to eat me," said Hector. "Mel, the others sent me to fetch you. We may have located Queen Morgause."

Mel turned immediately. She looked at Merlin. The old wizard smiled.

"Don't forget your bow, my young apprentice."

Mel grabbed her bow and her quiver of arrows and followed Hector out the door.

Merlin crossed the room. He lifted the stone Mel had levitated and turned it slowly in his hand.

Archimedes flapped and flew to his perch. He scowled at Merlin, then turned to the window and the red setting sun.

Erec, Magdalena, and Bors awaited Hector and Mel in the entrance hall of the castle. The Green Knight stood with them, munching on some mutton. Sir Lancelot and Sir Galahad, splendidly dressed, strode across the hall. Lancelot nodded.

"Magdalena . . . boys."

"What's the good word, Lancelot?" asked Erec.

A pause.

"Chivalry?"

"It's just an expression," said Erec. "How *are* you?"

"Well."

They waited but Lancelot said no more.

"Great. And you, Galahad?"

Galahad stared at Erec.

"Come along, Lancelot," sniffed Galahad. "The minstrels shall be starting soon. We've already seen *this* group's entertainment for the evening."

"What *entertainment*?" said Bors. "You mean saving Gawain from a great time-consuming prank?"

"Is that what you did?" said Galahad in a bored tone.

"I thought it was a pantomime."

"I have the feeling you don't appreciate our work," said Erec.

"I do not think you are anything special, no."

"We are best prepared for situations such as the Green Knight here," said Erec stiffly.

"Oh?"

"We have unusual experience."

"Such as?" asked Galahad.

"We fought an entire world of gigantic murderous lizards! You may recall that one? There were several songs written."

"Hmm. That so?"

"We battled monsters in the Orkneys," stated Bors. "And that was *at night*. In mist. Very low visibility."

"Again, there were songs," added Erec.

"Sorry. I do not pay much attention to gossip."

"Gossip!" Erec yelled. "We're living legends!"

Galahad chortled. "That's wonderful. Yes, you do jest most excellently, Sir Erec. Well done. But we must be off. Shall we, Lancelot?"

They swept from the hall.

"Git," said Erec.

Hector and Mel turned the corner.

"I have Mel! Say, have any of you ever been in Merlin's tower? He has thousands of books! I did not know so many even existed!"

"Fascinating, Hector," said Erec. "But we must prepare. At first light we are leaving to confront the Queen of Air and Darkness and bring an end to this adventure. Books will not help."

CHAPTER THREE

A MINUTE ON THE LIPS

The knights, Mel, and the Green Knight set out early the next morning. A few inches of snow covered the ground, and the bare trees stood out dark and skeletal against it. It was midwinter. *Bleak* was a good word to describe the scene.

The company rode in silence, all lost in their own thoughts. Sir Erec still bristled from the encounter with Galahad. Magdalena contemplated possible scenarios for capturing Morgause and, in particular, any tricks and traps that might await them in the faerie realm. Mel reviewed her recent magical training and her new skills and wondered whether any of it would be enough. She also thought of Morgause's son, Mordred, who was only two or three years younger than herself. Could he be saved from Morgause's hatred of Arthur, and her passion for revenge? Hector tried to focus, but he couldn't help dreaming about Merlin's library. Perhaps Merlin had some good books about gardening.

Bors was thinking about lunch.

"There," intoned the Green Knight from the front of the company. He was pointing at a most unusual house in the woods.

"What in Lancelot's name is that?" said Erec with a look of pure disgust.

"It's made of . . . ," began Hector.

"Rotting meat," finished Magdalena.

"To *you*." The Green Knight chuckled. "Yes, the house appears to be made of various rotting meats. But that is

a faerie trick. It has a very different appearance to its true
prey: children."

The Green Knight turned to Mel.

"My dear, most excellent Mel," he said. "You are not yet
too far away from that innocent time. What do you see?"

Mel squinted and tilted her head.

"It's blurry, but . . . it looks like the house is made of—"

"Sweets!" called Bors in delight. He dismounted and stomped toward the house. "Pies! Biscuits! Frosting! That house looks delicious!"

"Bors, you great oaf, stop!" bellowed the Green Knight. "If you take a bite of that house, you will be lost forever!"

"Forever?" asked Mel.

"Yes," said the Green Knight. "By no means *ever eat anything* in the land of Faerie. If you do, you will remain there for an eternity."

"But," said Bors, glancing at the chocolate window shutters.

"Bors, just don't bite the house. Not biting a house should be easy enough to remember," said Erec. "Right. So this is where we'll find Morgan Le Fay and Morgause. They are inside, Green Knight?"

"In a manner of speaking. You must proceed without me. I . . . I am not entirely welcome in parts of Faerie. The Good Folk and indeed some of the other Green Men feel that I spend too much time in the company of humans."

"Fair enough. We thank you for leading us here," said Erec, dismounting.

"Can't talk you out of it, can I?" asked the Green Knight.

"Nope," said Erec.

At the same time, Hector said: "Well, perhaps we should hear some of your reasons." He glanced guiltily at Erec, then added: "I mean, nope indeed."

"One more thing: you must leave your weapons here. No metal, especially iron, will be allowed to enter Faerie. The penalty will be swift and very unpleasant," said the Green Knight. "Very. Unpleasant."

"Can I bring my bow?" asked Mel.

"Yes, but not the arrows. Or, I suppose, the arrowheads," said the Green Knight.

"All right, then. Fellows, let us enter," said Erec.

He reached for the disgusting, rotten meat door and twisted the handle.

They entered. All was quiet and still. The one room of the house was bare of furniture of any kind. Thankfully, the interior was not made of meat, but of ordinary wood planks.

"I expected the realm of Faerie to be a bit more fantastical," said Erec.

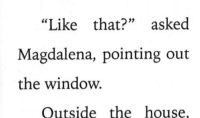

"Like that?" asked Magdalena, pointing out the window.

Outside the house, the surrounding area was no longer a bleak midwinter forest. The land was lush and green. The trees were gnarled and twisted with great roots snaking in and out of the ground. Strange and beautiful flowers and plants bloomed everywhere. The sky itself was an eerie pale yellow.

"Hmm," said Erec. "Back outside, I suppose. Be on your guard. And Bors, no snacking."

CHAPTER FOUR

WEIRD
SISTERS

Queen Morgause and her sister Morgan Le Fay sat at a long narrow table decorated with flowers and finely twisted vines in the center of a glen. Plates of luscious fruits, golden breads, and shimmering sweets filled the surface, along with goblets of nectar. At the center, a knight sat bolt upright and quite still except for occasionally lifting bread to his mouth and chewing slowly. He gazed into the distance in a perfect trance.

The two sisters paid him no mind. They were deep in conversation.

"You must always listen to your older sister, Morgan," said Morgause.

"My older sister is merely a visitor in Faerie and perhaps should listen to one who has experience here," said Morgan Le Fay quietly.

"Did I not seek you out? Did I not realize that the great and feared sorceress Morgan Le Fay could help me in my mission to destroy Arthur? I urge you to consider the wisdom of my plan."

"Is it wise to be so obsessed?" said Morgan. "To be consumed with revenge?"

"Our family has suffered greatly under Arthur and his father Uther before him. You once shared my thirst for justice."

Morgan looked at the dull yellow sky, the immense gnarled forest of Faerie.

"I have spent half my lifetime among the Good Folk here in Faerie. It changes you, dear sister."

"For the better, I assume," said Morgause. "At the very least you appear younger and more beautiful than last we met."

Morgan let out a short, mirthless laugh. "Time in Faerie has a strange effect on humans. Some grow old, some grow young. It is simply the surface. The real change happens inside."

"This past year has not harmed me, I can assure you," said Morgause.

"And your youngest son?"

"My *only* son," corrected Morgause.

"What of him?"

"Never better." Morgause smiled.

"Well, hello!" a third voice purred from the forest. A creature emerged, almost human in appearance. Thin. Otherworldly. His eyes, each a different strange color, were cold. He held a small baby wrapped in a blanket.

Morgause rose at the sight of him.

"Good day to you, Ash, King of All Faerie. I thank you once more for your hospitality, kindness, and benevolence."

"As you do every day," added Morgan under her breath.

"Ah. You used to say that to me every day as well, Morgan Le Fay. I miss it. Perhaps I will think of a new daily pledge for you. Wouldn't that be nice?"

Morgan did not respond. Ash turned his attention to the knight seated at the table.

"And how are we today?" he called, then laughed. "Oh, I forgot. You cannot speak. Perhaps one day I will allow you to rise from your banquet, brave knight." Ash turned to the sisters. "Imagine risking everything to save a mere baby. Knights and their quests! So earnest!"

Ash tossed the baby into the air. The sisters watched. The knight continued to eat, his eyes fixed in their blank stare. Several winged creatures caught the baby, tugging at the blanket. They giggled and murmured "yum, yum" over and over.

"Take it away, but do not eat it. Yet," said Ash with a lazy wave of his hand. The imps flew off.

Ash glided to the largest of the chairs. He put his feet up on the table.

"And so, Queen Morgause, let us talk more of your request."

"Gladly, Ash. I am anxious to begin. It *has* been a year and—"

"Do not bother me with the human measurement of time. It is silly and pointless. You humans understand nothing."

"Yes, Ash. That is true," said Morgause through gritted teeth. "I have much to learn from the Good Folk."

"Oh!" exclaimed Ash. "Endless knowledge! We are the most splendid beings."

"Exactly my point." Morgause gave him an ingratiating smile. "Why not add Camelot to your wondrous realm? Why limit yourself?"

"My dear, we are not limited. We come and go in the human realm as we please. We visit dreams. We haunt the woods. We are a flicker of movement in a mirror's reflection."

"Yes," said Morgause. "If they recognize your presence, to them it is occasional, a flutter, an abnormality. Like spotting a rainbow. People like King Arthur believe that *they* rule all."

"Well, that *is* silly," said Ash, taking a bite of some fruit. "Do you not think that is silly, dear knight?"

The knight took a bite of bread but still said nothing.

"Eat up, simple thing," Ash said as he tossed his own fruit into the woods. Small creatures swarmed over the scrap in an instant.

"Such foolish creatures, humans. Delusional kings. Baby rescuers. So easily tricked. Perhaps you are right, Morgause, and it is time for a change."

Morgause lit up. "Yes, Ash. With the Good Folk at my side—"

"You mean with you at our side."

"Yes."

"A little ways to the back."

"Yes, Ash, of course," said Morgause. "Together we will conquer Camelot. Who could possibly stop us?"

"HOLD IT!" cried Sir Erec as he and the others stumbled into the glen.

Morgause, Morgan Le Fay, and Ash turned to stare at them.

"Oh, for pity's sake," said Morgause.

"Queen Morgause," continued Erec. "There will be no conquering of Camelot on our watch. We insist that you come with us. You must account for your treachery and for unleashing monsters into the world."

"Especially for the monsters," added Hector.

"The creatures you call 'monsters' were already in the world, foolish knight. They are simply now common in *your* realm as well as theirs," said Ash patiently.

"And who are you?" demanded Bors.

Ash laughed. "I am Ash. I am wildness and uncertainty. I am wishes and dreams. I am of the earth and stars. I am—"

"Ash. Right. We get it. Are you in charge here?" asked Erec.

As the knights and Mel approached, Magdalena glanced at the spellbound knight. He raised the bread to his lips once more.

"In charge? I suppose you could say that," purred Ash.

"Then we ask your permission," said Magdalena, "to take Queen Morgause with us and return to our realm. By your leave."

"Oh, I do like you! Manners are so important. Are you, fair lady, a knight as well?"

"I am," said Magdalena.

"And you," said Ash, pointing to Mel, "are you a knight?"

"She is only a child," said a voice from the woods. A thin, teenaged boy with long, black hair stepped into the glen.

"Mordred?" asked Mel after moment.

"The same," said Mordred with a grin.

"Not the same at all," said Mel.  "Seeing as you were younger than me a year ago."

"Living in Faerie has its advantages. Time, age . . . those trifles can be changed if you wish," said Mordred.

"And you wished to be older?"

"I wished to reach my destiny."

"Right. You're coming, too, Mordred," said Erec.

"I think not. In fact, I do rather think that Ash might insist that you remain here," said Mordred.

"I am considering it," said Ash casually. He lowered his voice and addressed Mordred. "But do not ever presume to know what I am planning."

"Of course not, King Ash. I apologize. It is just that I would like to show some aspects of Faerie to Mel," said Mordred quickly. He turned back to Mel. "Some of the Good Folk share my interests in nightmare and torture. I get along very well with them. I believe the time has arrived for you to pay for what you did in Orkney."

Mordred moved with surprising speed toward Mel. Mel removed her bow from her back.

"Silly girl." Mordred laughed. "What good is a bow without arrows?"

As Mel aimed the bow and muttered a few words, it began to glow. Mordred was blasted into the air and thrown several feet back.

Ash clapped. "She knows a bit of magic! Well done! How delightful!"

Mordred got to his feet. His eyes were murderous. He rushed at Mel and she again raised her bow. Morgan Le Fay snapped her fingers and the bow became a snake, hissing and snapping. As Mel threw the snake, Mordred tackled her onto the table in front of the spellbound knight.

In the instant before anyone could act, Mordred raised a stone knife and thrust it down.

The spellbound knight's hand shot out and caught Mordred's wrist. The knife was mere inches from Mel's heart.

Ash leaped to his feet. "Foul knight! You were not under my spell! You tricked me! *Me!*"

Morgause quickly moved behind Morgan as Erec, Hector, and Bors tossed Mordred off Mel.

Magdalena faced Ash. "We are taking Morgause and Mordred. Now."

Ash's eyes flashed. "Did you really think it would be so simple?"

He brought his hands together with a sound like thunder.

And the knights and Mel were alone. Ash was gone. Morgause, Mordred, and Morgan were gone. The table was gone. The rotting meat house was gone. The woods had returned to normal. They were no longer in Faerie.

CHAPTER FIVE

NOW
WHAT?

Mel was the first to speak.

"Thank you, sir knight, for saving m—"

"You fools!" roared the mysterious knight. "You utter, complete fools!" He slammed his hand on a tree.

"Hold on," said Bors. "He was tucking in pretty well at that table. I thought you couldn't eat in Faerie."

"He wasn't really eating," said Magdalena. "Just sleight of hand. I noticed it as we passed the table. Very convincing."

"You do not need magic for deception," growled the knight.

"Who are you?" said Erec. "You're not from Camelot."

The knight's anger deflated into something else entirely.

"I am Sir Morien. The Good Folk still have the baby."

"Do not despair, Sir Morien," said Hector. "Your quest is not over."

"This is not a *quest*."

"A charge, then. Surely the baby's parents will understand if you need more time," offered Erec.

"She is *my* baby!" Morien erupted. And then, quietly: "*Our* baby. I was biding my time. Waiting for the moment to strike. She's so . . . scared. I was close. And now . . ."

Morien shook his head and wandered into the dark, ordinary woods.

"Sir Morien," called Mel. "We will help you return to Faerie."

"Let him go," said Magdalena.

"Poor fellow," said the Green Knight, who seemed to have materialized from the trees.

"Excellent," said Erec. "Green Knight, where is the meat house?"

"Right there," said the Green Knight, pointing to a clearing nearby.

"No, it's not. Nothing is there!" barked Bors.

"It is indeed, my foul-tempered friend," said the Green Knight. "You cannot see it, touch it, smell it, or hear it, but it is there. However, that way is no longer open to you."

"How do you hear a house?" wondered Hector.

"Enough riddles." Erec sighed. "We have no idea how long we have until this faerie invasion of Camelot. We need to find a glen or something with . . . I don't know . . . an unusual amount of moss."

"Faerie might find you, but you will not find Faerie. And yet, Faerie is everywhere," said the Green Knight.

"Your brain is moldy like your skin," said Bors.

"Let me try to explain," continued the Green Knight. "Think about the stars. Where are they in the daytime?"

Silence. Blank stares. The Green Knight tried again, more slowly.

"Work with me here. Where . . . are . . . the . . . stars?"

"Um," began Hector.

"Gone," said Bors flatly.

"No!" said the Green Knight with a beaming smile.
"They are still there in the sky!"

"No, no, no." Bors was not having it. "They are gone.

They are in the Star Place."

"The Star Place?" said Magdalena with raised eyebrows.

"How should I know what it's called!"

"The stars are still in the sky, Bors. You just cannot see them. Faerie is similar in a way."

More silence. Hector cleared his throat.

"You should see who is standing next to you at this moment, Hector," said the Green Knight with a wince. "Not pretty."

"Yes, well," said Hector, taking a hasty few steps to the right. "Perhaps we should go consult Merlin. He may know of another way into the faerie realm."

"Good idea," said Erec. "Although getting a straight answer out of Merlin is also unlikely. Mel, you better do the talking."

The knights and Mel mounted their horses and turned to go.

"Be careful, brave friends," called the Green Knight. "I fear you do not realize what you are up against."

"We never really do," said Erec as they rode off.

The journey back to Camelot was uneventful, but a strange mood had enveloped the castle. The few people around spoke in hushed tones. Some stopped speaking at the sight of Mel.

"Merlin," whispered Mel.

She took off, leaving the others confused. There was no time to tell them the story that Merlin had told her about the tree. A possibility, he said. Not a destiny. And yet . . .

Mel ran as fast she could up the curving stone steps to Merlin's tower, hoping he would be there, that she was wrong, that he had made a different choice.

She burst into the library. Merlin was not there. And the entire room—the books, the magical objects, the vials, globes, telescopes—*everything* was lifeless. Merlin's absence was total and complete.

"He's gone and done it. The old fool."

Archimedes the owl was perched by the windowsill, and he

was speaking to Mel for the first time.

"All of his incessant talk about possibilities and *reality* and *magic*, then he goes and does the *exact* thing he was warned of for years. 'Oh,'" the owl continued with a good impression of Merlin's voice, "'imprisoned in a tree for all eternity. What a nice vacation!'"

Archimedes ruffled his feathers. "What was the point of all this? What do we do now?!"

The owl fell silent. Mel was still stunned. Archimedes looked out the castle window before turning back to Mel.

"Well, I am through with humans and your illogical ways. No more will I stay in your company. From this day forward, if you by chance see me and call out, 'Hello, Archimedes!' I shall simply answer, *Who?*"

And with that the great owl flew through the window and far away from Camelot.

Mel glanced around the tower. Perhaps one of these books had a spell that could free Merlin from his imprisonment. Yes, she would search all . . . of . . .

the . . . books. No. There were far too many. And if such a spell did exist, it would take more than a novice's grasp of magic to cast.

After a quiet knock on the door, Hector stepped into the library. He walked over to Mel and stood beside her.

"If I'd been here, I could have stopped him," said Mel after a moment.

"I think . . . I think probably not, Mel," said Hector softly.

"It wasn't destiny or fate! He didn't have to go," said Mel angrily.

"Merlin made his decision. It is difficult to know someone's reasons. Merlin especially, I should imagine."

"I just want to *do* something."

"I know," said Hector.

"But I can't."

Hector sighed and sat down on a plush velvet sofa by the bookshelves.

"We can sit here," he said. "Together. It isn't much, Mel. But it is something."

Mel rubbed her eyes, then sat beside Hector. She leaned against his shoulder.

The two sat in silence for a very long time.

CHAPTER SIX

THE SQUIRES AND THE TREE

The next morning the band gathered in the hall by the kitchens of the castle to eat breakfast and discuss Next Steps.

Bors tucked into the full breakfast, Hector had his bread and jam, Erec concentrated on a stack of bacon and Magdalena on her scrambled eggs. Mel's untouched bowl of porridge cooled in front of her.

"All right," began Erec, crunching thoughtfully. "We have had some setbacks, but today is a new day and we are more than up to the task at hand. Who would like to start?"

Quiet munching sounds. Some soft sipping at cups.

"Start what?" asked Bors.

"Ideas. We are sitting here using our brains. I reckon we will have a veritable storm of ideas in just a few minutes," said Erec.

"Do *you* have an idea?" asked Hector.

"Certainly," said Erec. "I was just being polite and letting one of you go first."

More silence and stares.

"Yes. Well . . . ," began Erec. "A: we need to get back to the faerie realm. B: we must confront Morgause and this Ash creature. C: um . . . stop them from making Camelot part of the faerie realm."

"I think perhaps A is problem enough for now," said Magdalena.

"We go back to the forest, obviously," said Bors. "Wander around until we find some sort of magical creature and persuade it—roughly, I hope—to let us back into Faerie. There. Done! Plan set."

Bors sat back, quite pleased with himself.

"Well?" he continued. "Anyone have a better plan?"

"No," admitted Erec.

"Which is exactly our problem," finished Magdalena.

Mel stirred her porridge. "I have an idea," she said quietly.

"What is it?" asked Magdalena.

"We find a way to rescue Merlin. Merlin can stop Ash and Morgause."

Silence fell again. Mel began to eat, not looking up at the others. The knights exchanged glances, but none had any words for Mel.

"Well, look who it is!" rang out a voice.

Two knights in splendid attire strolled to the table.

"The Band of the Terrible Lizards! The Defenders of the Great Orkney Monster Scourge! Specialists in All Things Uncanny!" said the first knight.

"Hello, Tristan," muttered Erec. "And, of course, Lamorack. How is the sidekick business, Lamorack?"

"'Sidekick?' What is this you speak of? Sir Tristan and I are bosom companions. Friends of Adventure. We do not need a *band*."

"That's good," said Bors. "Since no one else can stand you two."

"Tut, tut, Sir Bors," said Tristan with a wide smile. "We are all friends here. We are Knights of the Round Table. Except for you," he said, pointing at Mel.

Tristan and Lamorack took seats at the table.

"Lamorack and I were just discussing some scuttlebutt we heard last night. Something about you lot failing to bring in Queen Morgause when you had the chance. Also something about an impending war with the Good Folk?"

"Who told you all that?" asked Erec.

"Uh . . . ," began Bors. "Well, I may have mentioned something about it last night over some mead in the Great Hall."

"Everyone is talking about it," said Lamorack. "That and Merlin's disappearance. I'm sure that was a blunder of yours in some way as well."

Mel raised her gaze. After only a brief moment, Lamorack looked away.

Tristan began to eat his breakfast. "It seems you have been a little . . . off for quite some time," he said, chewing. "I mean to say, for a long time you were all anyone talked about. Fighting giants and trolls and all sorts of scary creatures. Villages saved left and right. Practically nothing left for the rest of us to do."

"Do you want us to apologize for being exceptionally good at our work?" asked Erec.

"Of course not!" said Tristan. "You are brave and humble, Sir Erec. At least that is what all of the songs say."

Lamorack chuckled.

"But perhaps, Band of the Terrible Lizards, your glory days are coming to a close." Tristan finished his breakfast and stood.

"We will stop Morgause and the faerie folk, Tristan. Mark my words," said Erec.

"Hmm. By all means go out and try. But if you fail . . ."

Tristan and Lamorack strolled to the door. "Know that Camelot will always be protected by King Arthur's knights. Lancelot, Galahad, and yes, Tristan and Lamorack. We will never fail King Arthur."

"I should hope not, Tristan," said King Arthur, entering the hall. He was dressed in a riding cloak with thick, fur-lined boots and gloves.

"Sire!" Tristan and Lamorack fell to their knees.

"Remain as you were. Except for you, Mel. If you please, I would like you to accompany me," said Arthur.

"Anything we can do, my liege? Our swords are yours to command," said Lamorack.

"Thank you, no. Mel here will more than suffice."

Mel rose and dragged on her own cloak. Together, she and Arthur exited without another word.

"Mel's part of our band, you know," Erec said, munching his bacon.

A light snow fell as King Arthur and Mel rode silently out of the gates of Camelot. Mel wished she had time to find a new bow, but all she carried with her now was a knife. Then again, she was riding with King Arthur himself, who was armed with the magical sword Excalibur. King Arthur could surely rescue Merlin.

Mel studied Arthur as he rode ahead of her. So regal, so good. She could not say his age, but she had the strangest feeling, looking at him, that she could see a boy still in the man. A boy who knew more than he wanted to know. There was something about Arthur, especially today. Was it sadness? No, she realized.

Melancholy.

She thought about her own name. It was her mother's idea, apparently. Both of her parents had died before she was three, so she never asked her mother why she chose that name. The next family that took her on—*raised her* would not be the best way to describe it—never said anything about her parents. She had kept the name but shortened it to Mel, first to aid her as she disguised herself as a boy squire for Sir Bors, then simply because she had become used to it. She didn't often think about her full name these days. But it did seem to describe a deep part of her king.

They rode for a long time, the woods becoming thicker. Even covered in snow, the landscape seemed to hold mystery and uncertainty. She did not like these woods.

Arthur whispered a command, and his horse halted. He dismounted.

"Leave your horse here. She will not wander. We walk the rest of the way," said Arthur.

Mel climbed down, patted her horse, then joined Arthur. Together they trudged through the snow, down a hill, and into a small, secluded valley. Trees grew up the sides of the hills, towering above them. Arthur approached a solitary tree. It was thick and gnarled with great roots sunken into the ground. Its bark was a pale gray. It was both distinctive and strangely ordinary at the same time.

Mel stared at the tree and then at Arthur, who was also looking at it intensely.

"Is this . . . is this *the* tree?" asked Mel.

"Yes," said Arthur simply.

"Merlin is imprisoned in this tree?"

"I would not use that word myself. But, yes, this is where Merlin is now."

Mel approached the tree slowly. She reached out and placed a hand on the trunk.

"Do you feel anything?" asked Arthur.

"No," said Mel.

"Are you sure?"

"It's just a tree."

"Hmm," said Arthur in a vague way.

"Sire," said Mel. "What are we to do?"

"Do?" asked Arthur.

"To save Merlin."

Arthur smiled and said gently, "There is nothing we can do, Mel. But Merlin is still with us."

"You mean this tree?"

"No. I mean in here." He pointed to his head. "And here," he said, placing a hand over his heart.

Mel turned back to the tree.

"Merlin was my boyhood tutor," said Arthur. "He taught me all sorts of things, more than I thought I needed to know, since my future seemed destined to be serving as a squire for Sir Kay."

Mel looked at Arthur.

"Yes. I was a squire like you, Mel. Actually, I was not particularly good, so I was not like you at all, I suppose."

"You were not meant to be a squire," said Mel.

"No, it seems I was not," said Arthur quietly.

He fell silent for a minute or two.

"Merlin was a great believer in teaching by experience," Arthur began again. "As you well know by your adventure with the . . . uh . . . large lizards."

"Yes." Mel smiled. "That was indeed an experience."

"Merlin never made me do anything like that, of course." Arthur chuckled. "Though he did turn me into an ant once. That was very eye-opening."

They drifted into silence. Mel couldn't help picturing her great king as an ant.

"This is another experience, Mel. One that we must

face. And having faced it, we must move on with our lives, keeping this experience inside. It is part of us now. An important part."

Mel patted the tree again.

"And I suppose that for those who did not know Merlin, there will be stories of his deeds. He liked stories."

"Yes, he did," said Arthur, grinning. "We need not worry about Merlin in that regard. His legend will continue. He would have it no other way."

Arthur tilted his head up, taking in the entire tree. "But . . . I do hope that this tree might be forgotten. Give the old charlatan his peace and rest. His great holiday."

Arthur turned. "Come on, Mel. Let's get back to it."

Mel gave the tree a sad—no, *melancholy*—smile. Then she followed King Arthur back up the hill.

CHAPTER SEVEN

WHAT NOW?

Mel and Arthur returned to Camelot at midday. Mel took the horses to the stables, where she found her companions busy packing provisions for a long adventure. Erec saw Mel first and approached her.

"You all right?" he asked.

"Yes," said Mel with a nod.

"Merlin was quite a character. Irascible old trickster but . . . he did bring us together. I shall miss him," said Erec.

"So will I," said Mel, looking down.

"Well, we need to deal with this faerie invasion nonsense. If you want a break from your magical studies, we could sure use you."

"I am without a tutor. I'm afraid magic will need to wait for some time," said Mel. "Count me in."

"Splendid!"

Mel followed Erec. Bors, carrying a satchel of food, looked up as she approached.

"Good lad, er, lass," he said.

Mel laughed. Picking up another satchel, Mel caught sight of Magdalena strapping a saddle onto one of the horses. Magdalena looked up. She cleared her throat. She began to say something, but nothing came. Instead, she gave Mel a quick nod.

Mel nodded back and continued on. She passed Hector and patted him on the back.

"We have enough here for quite a long time," said Hector.

"As long as it takes," said Erec.

"Yes, well," Hector said, "let's hope it won't take *too* long."

They set off soon after. The immediate goal was to find

an entrance into the faerie realm. The Green Knight had wandered off to who knows where, but there were other supernatural creatures about these days. You just had to know where to look. Erec had an idea.

"There it is!" he proclaimed as the band halted on top of a hill overlooking a small village.

"That's a people village," said Bors.

"No, not the village. There." Erec pointed.

An ancient stone bridge crossed a stream below them. It was rather plain, but wide enough for a cart to cross. The arch beneath the bridge was dark and foreboding.

"I understand there is a troll living under this bridge. Some villagers asked if we could sort it out for them."

"When did they ask?" said Magdalena.

"Oh, several months ago," answered Erec.

"Several months?" said Hector.

"We have been busy," explained Erec. "Some requests get, you know, lost in the shuffle, as it were. However, we are here now, and I believe this creature can be of service." Erec urged his horse forward.

"Do trolls eat horses?" asked Mel. None of the others had moved.

"Goats, I think," said Hector.

Erec reined his horse to a stop.

"Good thinking. Let's not take any chances with the horses. On foot, everyone."

They all dismounted and ambled down the road. They crossed the bridge. Nothing happened. They walked back over the bridge. Still nothing. Bors tried stomping his feet as he walked.

"Trip, trip, trip!" he bellowed.

Erec peered over the side of the bridge. The arch below was deserted and unwelcoming.

"Maybe we should go down there."

"After you," said Hector.

Erec made his way down the slope to the edge of the water. Nothing but darkness under the bridge. Too much darkness, actually. No light whatsoever was visible, despite it being the afternoon.

"Hello!" he called.

No answer.

"Any trolls at home? We would like a word," tried Erec.

The others watched from above.

"We have a goat!" lied Erec.

The sound of shifting rock echoed from under the bridge.

A large, shaggy troll emerged from the darkness. "You woke me," he growled.

"Sorry," said Erec.

"It is winter," said the troll.

"Yes, it is. We need—"

"Don't you know that trolls hibernate?"

"No. I did not know that," said Erec, after a moment's thought.

"For how long?" Hector called down.

"Till I wake up!" barked the troll, stepping out from the arch and looking up. "How many of you are there?"

"Five," said Mel.

"Did you each bring a goat?"

"Ask him," said Magdalena, pointing at Erec.

"About that. What I meant to say is we will give you a goat or two if you answer our questions."

The troll straightened up. He was big. He was clearly not amused. Erec stumbled a bit, heading backward up the hill, followed by the lumbering troll.

"Questions?" the troll growled.

Erec hurried to rejoin the others.

"Weapons, I think," Erec whispered to the others.

The troll scaled the rest of the bridge. His head rested above the ledge. He took in the assembled company.

"Three questions?" the troll asked in a calmer voice.

"What?" asked Erec.

"Questions Three is traditional in my occupation," said the troll.

"All right. Sure. Just give us a second," said Erec.

The knights and Mel huddled and murmured among themselves. They broke.

"How do we get to the faerie realm?" asked Erec, holding up one finger.

"Do I look like a faerie? I am a bridge troll. We are completely different. I am offended, frankly," said the troll.

"But you all know one another, right?" blurted Bors.

"Oh! Sure! All the nonhumans know one another! Of course," said the troll sarcastically. "Very rude. *And* that was question number two."

"What—" Erec began, but Magdalena held up a hand to stop him.

They went back into a huddle.

Bors opened his mouth: "How—"

"*Shh!*" said the others.

They conferred again. A consensus was reached.

Erec approached slowly and very carefully asked, "If *you* were to contact the faerie realm, how would you do that?"

"Sleep," said the troll.

"Come again?" said Erec.

"That's four," grumbled the troll as he began to climb back down.

"No!" shouted Erec. "That was merely a request for clarification!"

The troll paused.

"Very well. I would go to sleep and dream. Dreams are sometimes a gateway into Faerie. That's it. I'll expect five goats by the morning. Thank you for your business."

The troll returned to the darkness beneath his bridge.

"Well, that was useless," grumbled Bors. "I'm not paying a goat for that," he added in a whisper.

"Sleeping," said Erec. "Great. He might as well have told us to look around until we found it."

"How would all of us get in through a dream?" pondered Hector. "We would all need to be having the same dream at the same time. That seems unlikely."

"I am glad you see the flaw in the plan, Hector," said Erec, sitting on the bridge wall.

"It will be dark soon," said Magdalena, heading back to the horses. "Let us seek lodging in the village for the night. Perhaps we will be lucky and dream our way to victory."

The others sighed and followed. Erec stayed behind for a moment to give the bridge a kick. For the first time he noticed a strange vine growing up the bridge. It was purple with deep crimson leaves. After a moment, he joined his companions.

CHAPTER EIGHT

THE PUNCH & PUNCHY SHOW

The knights and Mel made their way through the village and secured rooms at a ramshackle inn. Having stabled the horses, the band decided to take a stroll. Though small, the village had quite a few two-story wooden structures and a bustling atmosphere. There were open fires aplenty to warm passersby as the evening drew closer.

Walking down the narrow streets, they all kept quiet for the most part, each pondering the matters at hand. For Erec, Mel, Magdalena, and Hector, that meant the faerie problem. Bors was wondering about dinner. Turning a corner, they heard peals of laughter, both adult and child. A puppet theater had been set up in a square, and the show was in full motion.

Simple hand puppets spoke in comically high-pitched voices, and there was a lot of shouting and hitting involved. Each smack brought applause and laughter, so the puppets smacked often and well. On closer look, this was not the typical show featuring a rude and ugly married couple arguing about the baby. Instead, this show starred knights. Four knights. One was dressed entirely in black armor. One was on the stout side with a grotesquely large balding head and a bushy mustache. That puppet did the bulk of the squeaky yelling and hitting.

"How do they think of these things?" wondered Bors aloud.

Mel glanced up at him. She was about to offer some theatrical insight, but at that moment there was a great roar from the stage, and a crude lizardlike puppet started attacking the other puppets.

"Hang on," said Bors.

"Yes, it appears to be us," confirmed Hector.

The audience screamed with laughter. Occasionally the knights hit back, but the lizard was clearly the crowd favorite. It chased the knight puppets in a circle.

"It wasn't like that at all!" protested Erec.

Another, larger lizard puppet popped up and swallowed the knight puppets whole. The audience burst into applause.

"Honestly," grumbled Erec, "what passes for entertainment these days."

After a few moments' intermission, the puppet play began act two. The scenery was a barren moor. Powder was blown up from below, giving the illusion of mist.

"That is a good effect," said Magdalena approvingly.

The knight puppets reappeared to jeers and boos. A monstrous puppet popped up and scared the knights so badly that they all fainted over the side of the proscenium.

"I say," observed Hector, "we do not seem to be the heroes of this drama."

The monster puppet gobbled up the knights to tremendous laughter and applause. The curtain of the puppet theater fell. When the audience quieted down, the curtain opened once more. The knight puppets were gone. In their place was a small puppet of a girl with a quiver. She was trembling with fear.

A few chuckles came from the crowd, but as the puppet continued to quake, the laughter subsided. A greenish light shone on the puppet, and as it flickered, purple vines attached to rods began to crawl up from below and encircle the puppet.

Mel watched, hypnotized. Magdalena glanced sideways at her, then scowled at the stage.

A new puppet appeared in regal clothes of leaves, vines, and flowers. The puppet's painted face had the cruelest of smiles. When it spoke, its voice was low, melodic, and enticing, not the squeaky sound of the others.

"Come," the puppet called.

The curtain fell.

The audience burst into applause and started to disperse. No one noticed the presence of the puppet play's inspiration.

"It was pretty good up until the end," said Bors. "I didn't get the ending."

"Let us go back to the inn," said Magdalena.

And they did, Mel casting one last look at the puppet theater before joining the others.

They ate a simple dinner together at the inn. The long wooden table had been laid out with soup, bread, and a bit of cheese. Meager, but not terrible. The conversation was similarly meager.

"Those puppets got me thinking," said Hector, sipping his soup.

"Those puppets didn't know what they were talking about," grumbled Bors.

"They didn't talk at all," said Magdalena. "They just squeaked at one another."

"Yes, but the theme of the play led me to consider our

past and present situations," continued Hector. "When we battled the terrible lizards, it was in a land conjured by Merlin to teach us a lesson. Agreed?"

"Not sure about the lesson part, but yes," said Erec, crunching on some crusty bread.

"And that Orkney business with the monsters—" Hector shuddered. That adventure had included his own time *as* a monster and was still a sour memory. "When did the monsters show up?"

"Every night," said Bors. "Mist rolled in, and the monsters appeared."

"Precisely right, old friend," said Hector. "They came to *us* at a more or less regularly scheduled time. We knew they would come."

"I see what you are saying," said Erec. "Previously we did not have to do much to find trouble."

"But now we can neither find Faerie nor know with any certainty when the attack will come," finished Magdalena.

"Which is very, very annoying," said Bors, slurping the last of his soup.

"Fine. That is what we are facing. So what do we *do* about it?" asked Erec.

"Maybe . . . maybe this time there is nothing we *can* do about it," said Hector.

They all fell silent. The innkeeper approached the table.

"Anything else for you tonight?"

"No, I think not. Unless you know of a good, solid threat," said Erec.

"I do indeed know of a threat, but it is not solid," said the innkeeper.

Bors put his head on the table. "We're in no mood for riddles, innkeeper."

"Perhaps you have noticed that there's no one else at the inn," the innkeeper said.

The knights and Mel looked around the tavern, noticing for the first time the lack of customers.

"We have not had a single guest since the last day of October. That is when the hauntings became . . . enthusiastic."

"Hauntings?" asked Mel.

"Yes, miss. You may wonder how I remember the exact date so clearly?"

"No. But why?" said Erec.

"Because, Sir Erec of the Round Table and leader of the Band of the Terrible Lizards, the following day, November the first, is when I petitioned you to help rid us of our ghost problem."

"Petition? I don't recall a petition," said Erec.

"It was delivered to Camelot. I am sure you received it."

"Doesn't ring a bell."

"It looked, if I may, exactly like this," the innkeeper said, revealing a neatly written petition on fine parchment. "I copied and dated the petition before witnesses."

"How very thorough," said Erec, reading the petition. "I am sorry. We've been rather busy."

"Hmm," said the innkeeper. It was extraordinary how much rebuke he managed with such a small sound.

"Maybe that is why the villagers do not seem so keen on us," said Hector.

"A distinct possibility, Sir Hector," said the innkeeper icily.

"Well, we're here now. I don't see any ghosts," said Erec.

"You will, Sir Erec. And so, if I can do no more for you, I shall retire for the evening. Next door," added the innkeeper.

The band headed up the stairs to their rooms. Mel and Magdalena were in the small attic bedroom, and the others were together in the larger room on the second floor. All were very interested in experiencing a real haunting. But waiting for ghosts proved to be rather dull. Eventually they all laid down in their beds and rested while they waited. Mel was the first to fall into a deep sleep.

CHAPTER NINE

NIGHT WANDERINGS

At first, Mel didn't dream at all. She slipped deeper and deeper into a comfortable sleep. Drifting and drifting.

Until . . .

She was in the village square, standing before the puppet theater. There was no one else in the street. The small Mel-like puppet stared from the stage. It laughed.

And then . . .

Mel was *on* the puppet stage, standing next to the puppet that was now her exact size. Mel turned toward the back of the stage. Trees were painted very simply on the backdrop. A breeze blew, and the puppet had gone. The painted trees seemed more vibrant and almost lifelike.

Mel began to walk, and the painted backdrop was no longer a simple canvas. Had it ever been? She was in a real forest, but a very strange one. Tall, thin, gnarled, and twisted, the trees curled up and around her, creating a complicated canopy blocking a green-gray sky. Purple vines coiled around the trunks. The leaves were many shades of lush green, and yet the ground was covered with orange and red leaves as if it were autumn.

Small lights darted toward her. One flew very close, and Mel could see that the glowing creature had long spindly arms and legs, eyes set close together, and large, heavy

jaws that seemed at odds with the delicacy of its wings.

It bit her.

"Ouch!" said Mel. She had felt the bite. Yet this was a dream. Nothing to worry about. Sometimes the mind tricked you in dreams, made you "feel" a sensation even if it was not true.

A second winged creature grabbed her hair and pulled. Mel swung for it but missed. She wished she had her bow but no, arrows were not allowed. Never any iron here. Of course not. That would be very, very wrong!

Mel kept walking through the woods, swatting at the flying creatures, until she realized she was swatting at nothing. They had gone.

But she was not alone.

"So nice of you to join us, Melancholy." Ash stood a few yards away.

"This is just a dream," said Mel.

"Yes. No. What does it matter? Will you walk with me?"

Mel could not think of a reason to refuse, so she joined the faerie king.

"I have been hearing so much about you," said Ash. "Morgause and Mordred do not seem to like you, but that is not of any concern. I reach my own conclusions."

Faeries of all shapes and sizes lurked at the edge of the shadows, but Mel did not feel threatened.

She was intrigued by each new creature.

"I do believe you would be an excellent addition to my collection," said Ash.

That snapped her out of it.

"Your *collection*?"

"Yes. It is quite delightful," said Ash. "Some I steal, such as the baby; some I trick; and some, some come to Faerie willingly. Those are my favorites."

"And what happens to them when they come to Faerie? What do you do with them?"

"Do? Nothing. I simply collect."

"Are they happy?"

"Why should I care about their happiness?"

They entered a grand hall that was stunning in its strangeness. There were walls but no ceiling. The purple vines snaked across the floor and over tables that were laid with the most delicious-looking food Mel had ever seen. She was *so* hungry.

Night had fallen, and the hall was lit by a million sparkling dots of light that hovered and darted about the sky. At the far end was a great door, the only door Mel had seen in Faerie.

I should want to go through that door and escape, thought Mel. But she did not want to just yet. She wanted to listen to the ethereal music that was playing softly. Perhaps Faerie was not so terrible. . . .

"Not so terrible at all," said Ash.

Mel turned to Ash, alarmed.

"Do not worry," said Ash with a chuckle. "This is only a dream, is it not, Melancholy?"

"Yes," said Mel. "Only a dream."

"You might as well enjoy it. Have a bite to eat." Ash held out a luscious ripe fruit.

Mel reached for it but . . but . . .

"No!"

Mel fell out of her bed. At the inn.

Magdalena sat up in the bed next to Mel.

"I'm fine," said Mel.

Magdalena lay back.

"Not that you asked," added Mel in a whisper. She

glanced down at her hand. A bracelet of purple vine was wrapped tightly around her wrist. Mel covered it with her sleeve.

The door burst open. Bors bounded in, fists held high, a feverish look on his face.

"Where is it?"

"Where is what?" asked Mel.

Magdalena pointed across the room. "There," she said.

Hovering above the floorboards was the transparent figure of a sad-faced man.

"AHH!" roared Bors as he threw himself in an attempt to tackle the ghost. He sailed straight through and hit the wall.

"Ooh! Cold!" he grumbled. The ghost calmly floated back out the door.

"Oh no you don't!" Bors took after the ghost.

Magdalena and Mel exchanged a look, then followed. The hallway of the inn was quite a scene. Hector was surrounded by ghosts, and he appeared to be trying to soothe them. Erec, on the other hand, was swinging his

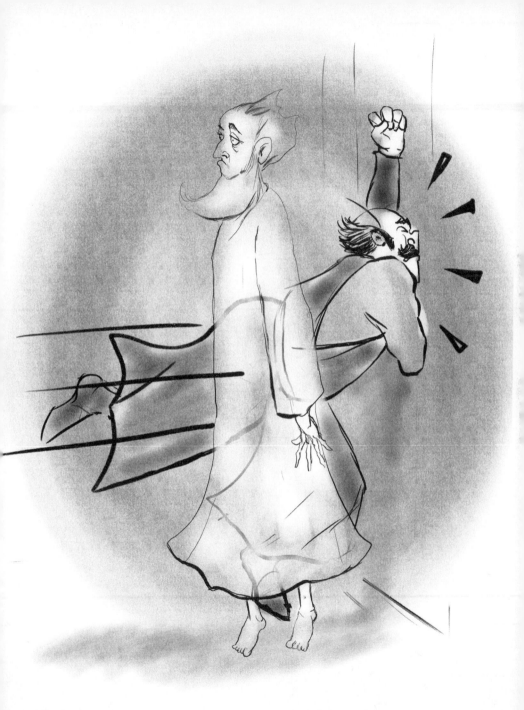

sword wildly on the stairs, dueling with another specter. Every time Erec's sword slashed, it went right through the ghost's sword.

"This . . . is . . . not . . . fair!" huffed Erec.

More ghosts were materializing out of the walls and floorboards, the cabinets and cupboards. They were men and women, old and young. They were completely silent and rather placid for the most part.

"Try to lead them downstairs," called Magdalena.

The band slipped down the stairs. The ghosts watched, then drifted down behind them. They all

ended up in the dining room of the inn, knights and Mel in one corner, several ghosts floating as a pack in the other.

Bors was in the center of the room, still fighting with a portly ghost who simply stared as Bors punched and punched.

Finally Bors, completely out of breath, slumped down

on a bench by the others and scowled. Everyone else took a seat as well. The ghosts hovered.

The hours passed. The two sides remained exactly in place, no words spoken, no movement except for the gentle rising of the ghosts.

Dawn came, and as the first ray of sunlight slipped into the room, the ghosts simply faded away.

The innkeeper unlocked the front door and joined them.

Erec stood and clapped his hands. "Well! That takes care of that!" he said rather too loudly. "Your ghosts have been dealt with."

"Dealt with?" the innkeeper asked.

"Yes," said Erec.

"They won't reappear tonight?"

"Er . . . no," said Erec.

"Are you sure? They always vanish in the daylight."

"This time it's different." Erec turned to the others and lowered his voice. "Time to move on."

"What shall I do if the ghosts return?" asked the innkeeper.

"Good-bye!" Erec smiled.

The knights shuffled out the door sheepishly, not making eye contact with the innkeeper. No one spoke until they reached the stable.

"I don't know how to fight a ghost," said Erec finally. "I don't know how to help that innkeeper."

The others remained silent.

Erec lifted his saddle roughly. "Villagers are making puppet jokes about us. Galahad and Tristan and their ilk look down on us as has-beens."

"So what do we do?" asked Mel.

Erec saddled his horse and paused.

"We stop this faerie king. He is flesh and bone. He can be beat. And that is exactly what we are going to do."

CHAPTER TEN

THREE
IMPS

"Where do we go now?" asked Bors.

They were standing in a circle of trees. At the base of each trunk, twigs, pine cones, and other natural debris had been arranged to resemble tiny dwellings or entranceways.

"Yes. It would seem that these are *not* in fact faerie houses, as we were told," said Erec in a stony voice.

Hector, kneeling beside one, lifted a toadstool. "Whimsical, though," he said.

"Whimsy is useless," said Erec, kicking one of the dioramas.

They had searched for weeks, following leads and rumors of faerie activity. This adorable display of folk art was the closest they had come to success.

"It will be evening soon. We should camp here," said Magdalena, unpacking supplies from her horse.

"I'll start the fire," said Mel, happy to have a simple, straightforward task to accomplish. She walked deeper into the woods to gather kindling.

"Ooh," said Hector. "This one has a little balcony! Come see, Bors!"

Bors gave Hector a long look, then turned to his horse to remove the blankets.

Mel wandered to the bank of a stream. The water rushed intensely, pushing plates of melting ice against the rocks. She lifted her sleeve. The purple vine now covered most of her forearm. It was growing, slowly, steadily, imperceptibly.

A strange feeling came over her. Across the stream, high on a hill, stood Ash, the faerie king. He was watching her.

Mel froze. Should she call the others? *No*, a voice inside her head answered. But it was not her voice.

She hadn't turned and couldn't recall even blinking, yet Ash was no longer on the hill. Was it a trick of the light?

"No."

This time the word was a whisper, right at her ear. Mel spun, and there was the faerie smiling broadly.

"Tonight, Melancholy," said Ash.

Then, in a strong gust of wind and a whirl of snow, Ash was gone.

Mel calmed her breathing. She was not entirely sure she had actually seen Ash. That was extremely troubling in itself. Mel was confident in her powers of observation, her cool head, her . . . her *Mel*-ness.

She checked the ground where she stood. No tracks, but that was not surprising.

"You all right?" asked Erec when she returned to camp.

"Hmm?" said Mel.

"You seem a little—"

"I'm fine. Thinking is all." She smiled at Erec,

then arranged the wood by the firepit. She glanced at Magdalena, who was busy setting up a short distance from her. Mel closed her eyes, concentrated, and murmured a spell she had learned from Merlin, and the fire ignited at once.

Merlin. She could have told him what she had seen. But why not the others? Mel had no real answer. Somehow it seemed as though she needed to deal with this alone. She cast another look at Magdalena, who was still occupied with setting up the camp.

"Bors!" Hector called from the circle of trees.

"Hector, I do not care about your little stick dollhouses. I do not care if there is a balcony, drawbridge, moat, or even a teensy dungeon," grumbled Bors.

"On the count of three, catch it," said Hector.

"Catch what?"

"One, two, three!" Hector kicked the trunk of a tree, and something much too large for the decorative window flew out. It had long, gangly arms and legs with dragonfly wings. It zoomed toward the campsite.

Bors lunged and caught it. The creature sank razor-sharp teeth into his hand.

"Yow!"

It flew from his hands and hovered just out of reach.

"Do not touch Crumpet, you smelly man!" squeaked the creature.

Everyone stared at Crumpet.

"Have you never seen an imp before?" Crumpet demanded.

"No," answered Mel for everyone. And yet it *did* seem familiar.

"Oh!" said Crumpet. "Now you will see three! Blister! Scab!"

Two more imps squeezed out of the faerie houses and flew over.

"Are they the ones?"

"I do believe so, Blister," said Crumpet. "What think you, Scab?"

Scab flitted over to Erec. It bit him on the neck.

"Hey!" yelled Erec, swatting at the imp.

"Yes!" said Scab. "He tastes like I thought he would. Yum."

"You are the humans who disrupted the faerie king's banquet. That was unwise!" accused Blister.

"Why don't you tell us how to return so we can apologize?" said Erec.

"An apology would be nice," said Crumpet, "but *useless!*"

"Tell us how to get there anyway," said Bors.

"No, no, no, no," sang the three imps as they flew in circles around the knights.

Magdalena grabbed at one, but even she was too slow.

"How about a riddle of some sort?" interjected Hector. "We answer correctly and you show us the way. I believe you faeries enjoy that sort of thing."

The imps paused in midair, considering the offer.

"No, no, no, no, no, no, no," they cackled.

"Yum!" Scab added for good measure.

"We will not show you the way. Though perhaps *you* already know it?" Crumpet shot a look at Mel.

The imps soared around once more, pulling hair and taking quick bites at everyone before zipping into the woods, glowing like enormous fireflies.

No one spoke. Finally they had found a solid lead, and it had just flown away. Laughing at them.

Bors kicked a pine cone house away from a tree.

The band stayed put, hoping that the imps might return. They ate and spoke little. Failure hung over the camp. Failure and frustration and fatigue. Eventually they slept.

Mel woke soon after, but not at the campsite. She was once again in the grand hall in Faerie. Faeries of all sorts danced merrily to strange, hypnotic music. The air was warm, and all of the flowers were in full bloom. Mel walked slowly, not exactly afraid, but certainly cautious.

"Welcome," said Ash, who was suddenly beside her. "Hungry?"

Mel didn't answer.

"Oh, you are the clever one." Ash chuckled. "Later, perhaps? Shall we visit the others?"

He led Mel to a corner furnished with enormous velvet chairs and chaise lounges. Morgause and Morgan Le Fay sat. Mordred stood a short distance away.

"Why is she here?" said Morgause with dislike.

"Because I wish her to be here," said Ash. "She, too, wishes to be here."

"I do not," objected Mel.

"And yet you came." Ash grinned.

"I am not here. I am dreaming."

"You are half-correct," said Ash, stretching out on a chaise. "You are dreaming. But you *are* here."

Ash nibbled a grape and considered it for a moment.

"Then again, you are also not here. So you are two-thirds correct. Not bad for a mortal. You will be such an excellent addition to my collection."

Mel went cold, despite the crackle of the fire.

Mordred stared at her with quiet loathing.

"These two," said Ash, gesturing at Mordred and Morgause, "are impatient for me to conquer Camelot and vanquish King Arthur. What say you, Melancholy?"

"I think you should *not* do that," said Mel. "We will stop you."

"'We?'" Ash chuckled. "There is nothing any of you can do."

A baby began to cry. Sir Morien's baby. Ash approached an enormous flower where the baby lay.

Mel had to do something. She had to save the baby. She must—

Morgan Le Fay was at her side.

"Wake," she hissed.

Mel woke by the fire. Her companions slept around her. The forest was dark and cold and silent. There was no crying baby.

CHAPTER ELEVEN

DREAM, KICK, DUEL

The spring thaw began, but instead of bringing a feeling of renewal, the growing buds had a slightly ominous look. The company searched forest, glens, lakes, caves—everywhere—but there were no signs of the faerie realm.

Except for the purple vines. Every day there were more, choking tree trunks and crossing paths.

"These blasted vines," said Erec. "Have you noticed?"

"They are spreading in the same direction," said Hector.

"Toward Camelot," said Magdalena.

It was late afternoon. The band had stopped in another forest. Mel wandered off to think. She had returned to Faerie only once more in a dream. She had watched the faerie celebration from a distance. No one spoke to her. She did not see Ash or the others. Yet this dream was the most disturbing, for she'd *longed* to join in the celebration.

Mel felt more alone every day now. Magdalena, her one-time teacher, barely spoke to her. Was the Black Knight disappointed Mel neglected archery to dabble in wizardry? Was Magdalena just finished with her now? The distance between them grew, often literally. As Mel sat and pondered, Magdalena had ridden on alone to search for signs. She had left without a word, of course.

There were quite a few words coming from the other three members of the band, however. Some not suitable for repeating.

Bors was having a heated argument with a tree.

"He's completely lost it," Erec said to Hector.

Bors, red-faced, was pointing a finger at the old tree. A gnarled bit of bark on the trunk had a passing resemblance to a bearded face.

"I'm on to you, tree! Open up!" yelled Bors.

"I can sort of make out a face," said Hector, squinting from a safe distance away. "It takes more imagination than I thought Bors possessed, poor fellow."

"Fine! We do it the hard way!" roared Bors, and he kicked the tree.

"Ooh," said Erec. "That hurt."

Bors was not beaten. He began to pummel the tree with his bare fists.

Erec sighed.

"Erec," began Hector over Bors's grunts. "Have you ever thought about . . . well . . . we've been at this for quite a while now."

"You want to give up our search for Morgause and the faerie king?"

"Of course not," said Hector quickly. "But *after* we've stopped them . . ."

"Are you talking about quitting? No more adventure? No more knighthood?"

"Well, just a simpler life for a change. Still keeping busy, you know. But perhaps fewer . . . evil creatures and things like that," said Hector.

Erec sputtered a bit, but couldn't form any actual words.

"Vile villain! I will make you talk, Tree Man!" Bors kicked the tree again and then hopped around holding his toe.

"This is perhaps not our finest hour," said Erec quietly.

Magdalena rode slowly through the woods on her great midnight-black steed. The horse snorted.

"I am bored as well, my old friend," said Magdalena.

She halted her horse and scanned the surrounding forest.

"No sign of faeries here." Magdalena patted her horse. "But at least I'm having a nice ride with you."

The horse whinnied.

"Yes, and a nice talk. It has been a while since we chatted."

Magdalena flicked the reins, and they continued on.

"Why is it so easy to speak with you and so difficult sometimes with the others?"

Snort.

"I know it's ridiculous. But conversation has always been a challenge for me."

The horse shook its mane.

"Mel? Yes, even with Mel nowadays. Of course, my counsel and teaching *should* be coming to an end. It is right that she finds her own way."

The horse bucked a little, jostling Magdalena in the saddle.

"No. I am sure I am correct. Mel doesn't need . . ." The words trailed off. Magdalena wiped her brow, then brought the horse to a halt. She sniffed the air. Campfire, extinguished, maybe a few hours ago. She dismounted and tied the reins around a low tree branch.

The horse whinnied softly.

"Thank you," said Magdalena, patting the horse's neck. "It is always good to talk with you, too, Peaches."

Magdalena moved cautiously through the trees until the landscape opened up to a hillside filled with boulders and rock formations. A little ways up was a cave. In front of the cave was Sir Morien.

He was still as stone himself, his back to Magdalena. She took a silent step closer.

"Leave me," said Morien without turning.

She took another step.

"Leave me now, be you friend or foe. I have no time for you."

Magdalena took a deep breath.

"How long now?" she asked.

Morien slowly turned his head. He regarded Magdalena.

"Six months. Six months since our baby was spirited away. Two months since I last saw her. When you and your companions ruined my plan."

"We did not know."

"It matters not."

Magdalena approached and stood a few feet behind him, watching the cave.

"Have you found an entrance to Faerie?"

"Possibly."

Silence fell.

"I have heard of you, Sir Morien," said Magdalena. "I have heard of your bravery and skill. For six months a knight of action has been forced to wait with nothing to strike, nothing to smite. I cannot offer you much; we have not been successful either. But I offer this: fight me, brave knight.

Just for a while hit something concrete that will hit you back. Direct some of your anger at me."

Magdalena drew her sword. She waited.

Morien spun, drew his sword, and struck. Magdalena barely managed to block the blow. Morien thrashed again. Clang! Clang! Magdalena backed up to the rock wall. Then with one mighty swing, Morien achieved the unimaginable: he knocked Magdalena's sword from her hand. Morien's blade stopped inches from Magdalena's throat.

"You think me angry?" said Morien quietly. "I assure you, Black Knight, I lost my anger a long time ago."

Sir Morien lowered his sword and

returned to his place at the mouth of the cave. "Now there is only *fury*."

Magdalena retrieved her sword and left Morien without another word. She returned to camp with a cut on her cheek.

"What happened to you?" asked Erec.

"Sir Morien and I dueled."

"Oh," said Erec. "Who won?

"Morien," said Magdalena.

Silence. The other knights turned to Magdalena.

"Is he joining us?" asked Hector.

"No," said Magdalena.

Mel started the fire with her spell. She watched the Black Knight. Magdalena held her eye for a split second, then turned to the fire.

Bors leaned against the gnarled tree. He gave it one more punch, but it was halfhearted, at best.

"I miss the monsters and the lizards," he muttered.

CHAPTER TWELVE
CHOICES

"**M**elancholy."

Ash's voice called, but this time not in a dream. Mel woke. Her companions slept around the low-burning fire.

"Melancholy."

The voice traveled as if on a breeze. Mel sat up. The three glowing imps perched in a tree, staring at Mel. They alighted and drifted into the woods. Mel stood. She paused a moment to look down at the others.

They had been through much together, but now—she

was sure of this—now she must go on alone. Ash wanted her for some reason. Maybe she could set at least one thing right. Weaponless, Mel followed the light of the imps into the dark wood.

"She is here!" said Crumpet as they entered a clearing that brushed up against thicker, denser woods. It gave the impression of a stage or amphitheater.

Ash stood in the clearing, smiling.

"Wonderful," Ash said.

And then Sir Morien stepped from the shadows, his sword raised.

"Tedious." Ash sighed.

"I shall fight to the death," said Morien.

"No. Wait, Sir Morien. King Ash, I have a bargain for you," said Mel.

Ash still grinned, but his demeanor was suddenly colder.

"*If* Sir Morien's baby is returned immediately and never taken again," Mel continued, "I will come willingly with you."

"Interesting," said Ash.

"I may not be able to stop you or save Camelot. But I *can* save the baby," said Mel.

"And you will stay in Faerie?" asked Ash.

"Forever," said Mel.

Ash chuckled. "Oh, let's not be dramatic. I am a fair faerie. Let us just say . . . *until the impossible comes to pass.* That has a nicer ring to it."

The baby appeared with a sparkling light, wrapped in a beautiful green blanket, set safely on the grass.

Morien sheathed his sword as he rushed to the spot. He paused, inches from his small child.

"Mel," said Morien.

"It's all right, Sir Morien. Please, take your baby and go far from Camelot," said Mel more firmly.

Morien picked up the baby, who gave a small giggle at the sight of him. Morien was lost for a moment, staring at his daughter.

"Thank you," breathed Sir Morien.

Erec, Magdalena, Bors, and Hector plunged out of the forest. "STOP!"

"A bargain has been made," said Ash with a smile. "Just to save a baby. How very strange."

Magdalena drew her sword as Mel went to Ash's side.

"You have a strategy, right, Mel?" said Erec frantically.

"Not this time," said Mel.

The world seemed to blur. When it came back into focus, Mel and the faerie king were gone.

CHAPTER THIRTEEN

THE FURY OF THE BLACK KNIGHT

"**R**RRRAHH!"

It was all Bors could say.

Hector and Erec raced to where Mel had stood, searching for . . . anything.

Sir Morien stepped forward, holding his baby.

"I am sorry for you," he said. "However, my heart is filled with joy. I do hope sincerely that you someday find a way to Mel. Her sacrifice means all the world to me and my family. She will not be forgotten."

No one spoke.

Morien turned and walked to the edge of the clearing, where his horse waited. He mounted with the baby held close.

"I regret that I cannot stay," Morien said.

"No," said Magdalena. "You must leave Camelot for your little girl. Her childhood will be a great adventure. I daresay you would not want to miss it."

"Not for the world," said Sir Morien, and he turned his horse and rode off.

"Right," said Erec, snapping back into action. "Find those imps. Cratchet, Boil, and Pus or whatever their names are. We will force them to—"

"Mel vanished here. Perhaps we should stay. Perhaps the way into Faerie lingers for a time," interrupted Hector.

Magdalena stood stock-still, her gaze fixed on the spot Mel last stood. She breathed slowly, evenly. She closed her eyes, then opened them, scanning the trees and the surrounding area. She walked along the edge of the tree line.

"*RRRRRAHH!*" roared Bors.

"Be quiet, Bors," said Magdalena.

"Quiet? *Quiet?* I think hollering is a perfectly normal response. Unlike you, Magdalena, I am not cold and silent as a stone! This is not the time to be calm and cool and quiet!"

Magdalena turned to Bors and spoke softly. "I am neither calm nor cool. *Mel* has been taken. I am *furious.* Now. Be. Quiet."

Bors, Hector, and Erec watched Magdalena in silence.

She breathed slowly and turned back to the trees.

Meanwhile . . .

In Faerie, Ash sat on a throne in the great hall with Mel at his side. The hall had a single wooden door at the opposite end. Torches cast a strange green light on the throne and the door, but the rest of the hall was in shadow.

Mel glanced down at her left wrist. The purple vine that had been twisting around her arm turned to dust and blew away in a breeze.

"I do so love it when I get what I want," said Ash.

"You didn't get the baby," said Mel.

"True. But I no longer wanted the baby. My mood changes often. One whim today, another tomorrow. Sometimes I do not even *look* the same. You will get used to it," said Ash. "You will have no choice," he added.

In the forest . . .

Magdalena stood before two gnarled, twisted trees that stood six feet apart. Her eyes climbed the trees. She rested a hand on the trunk of one and then the other.

Bors, Hector, and Erec watched, puzzled.

Magdalena made a fist, drew it back, then thrust it into the empty air between the trees.

BOOM!

Ash and Mel turned toward the great door at the far end of the hall.

"What was that?" asked Ash.

BOOM!

Magdalena raised both fists and pounded the air between the trees.

BOOM!
BOOM!

Ash stood slowly.

"No," he whispered.

Silence.

And then the great door burst open with one final

BOOM!

The Black Knight stood in the doorway.

"That is . . . ," said Ash.

"Impossible," finished Mel.

Ash waved a hand at Mel, and vines crawled from her chair to bind her. He snapped his fingers and creatures of all kinds appeared from the shadows and scurried down the walls, an army of monstrous beings.

Magdalena had not moved. She simply stared directly at Ash. Her eyes were terrifying.

Ash laughed.

"She does not even have a weapon!" he chortled.

Mel met Magdalena's eyes.

"She won't need any," said Mel.

The creatures of Faerie attacked.

And the Black Knight . . .

Magdalena crossed the hall, stepping over the vanquished foes. She took a faerie knife, carved from a thorn, and cut through the vines that held Mel.

"You came for me," said Mel.

Magdalena paused. She turned to Mel.

"I will always be there for you. No matter what. As long as you need me. As long as I live."

Mel wiped her eyes and smiled. Magdalena smiled back.

"Now let us get out of this strange, unpleasant place," she said.

"Gladly," said Mel.

There was a great clattering at the door, and Hector, Erec, and Bors tumbled in.

"Good! Excellent!" cried Erec. He examined the hall of fallen enemies. "Did you do all of this?"

"Of course she did," said Bors. "I'd recognize her work anywhere."

Hector was still by the door. "We're not out of the woods yet. . . . Actually it appears that our woods have vanished. We need to find another escape route."

"Let's go!" said Mel.

Outside the hall more faeries, elves, goblins, and creatures without name were gathering.

"There are more of them," called Hector.

"I should hope so," barked Bors, and he threw himself into battle.

The heroes fought with all their might. Weeks of frustration, anger, and fear poured out and was directed at the Good Folk of Faerie. Having left their swords behind, they made do with fists and kicks, clubs and borrowed faerie weapons.

A safe distance away, Morgause, Mordred, Morgan Le Fay, and Ash pondered the scene.

"They are really quite good. At fighting, I mean," Ash mused.

"Inexplicably so," said Morgause.

Ash sighed.

"That Black Knight is something. I should have taken *her*."

"I do not think that would have ended well," said Morgan Le Fay.

Ash shot her a look. She turned away.

"No. Perhaps not. Speaking of ending," Ash continued brightly, "I believe this has gone on long enough."

"Kill them all," said Mordred with an intense gleam in his eye.

"Tsk, tsk," said Ash. "Such brutal language. I do not care for you, Mordred. You utterly lack style."

Ash turned again to the battle. "This is how it shall end." He clapped twice and the sound was deafening.

All of the fighters stopped. A shadow passed over them. Faeries and knights alike looked to the sky.

"Oh crikey," said Erec.

A dragon, a real dragon, swooped over them, screeching a horrendous call. Its long serpentine neck whipped toward the crowd.

The dragon was not particular. It managed to devour a dozen goblins on its first pass. The Good Folk scattered, clambering into the woods or scurrying down holes.

The dragon landed with a tremendous thud in front of Bors, Hector, Erec, Mel, and Magdalena. It bared its teeth. It swished its great tail.

"All right," said Erec. "We have dealt with similar creatures before. Let us do what we do best."

The dragon lunged and the heroes split up. Magdalena ran for the dragon's neck. Bors and Hector, clubs in hands, struck at its head. Mel attempted to run beneath the wings with an idea of climbing onto its back. Erec went for the underbelly with a thorn knife.

They were all knocked back easily. Mel hit the ground hard.

The dragon took to the sky, then plunged again, heading straight for Mel. In an instant Bors was there, standing solid as a rock in front of her. The dragon lifted him into the air as Bors pounded its snout. Mel scrambled to safety.

The dragon shook Bors and spat him back down to the others, before lifting off to the sky.

But not *all* of him.

Bors was missing one leg.

CHAPTER FOURTEEN

THE END
IS NIGH

Bors was very, very angry about his leg.

Mel ran to Bors's side immediately, and the others joined within seconds. They formed a protective circle around the fallen knight.

"There must be a spell to stop the bleeding!" Mel ripped a strip of cloth from her tunic and tied it around Bors's leg. "There is! I read about it . . . can't . . . remember . . ."

Bors paused his tirade of curses and put his hand on Mel's arm.

"Calm down, Mel. It's all right," Bors said. "You have a bigger problem right now."

The dragon screeched, circling back toward them with powerful beats of its wings.

And then there was a new sound: a low, rumbling tone like music but more elemental. It sounded, if such a thing was possible, ancient like Time itself.

The Green Knight, followed by a hundred more Green Men, some more tree than man, approached the dragon.

The dragon recoiled. It spat a few flames but inched back. The Green Men sang and stood before the dragon, protecting the knights and Mel. The song rose in volume to a near-deafening rumble. The dragon flinched before soaring high up into the sky and flying away.

The song ended. The Green Knight turned to Ash, who stood by the forest edge. The faerie king scowled at the Green Knight, then shimmered away.

The Green Knight and another Green Man hurried to Bors's side.

"Well done, Froggy," said Bors weakly. "I didn't know you could sing."

"I will give you a lesson one day," said the Green Knight. "But first we must take care of this wound."

The Green Knight's companion produced a large, emerald-green leaf.

"A leaf?" asked Bors.

"A magical leaf," said the Green Man.

"Oh. By all means, leaf me up," groaned Bors.

"Can you save the leg?" asked Magdalena.

"No. But he will have a fine, healthy stump," said the Green Knight with a wink.

"A fine stump," agreed the other Green Man.

"Ash is gone. They're all gone," said Erec, checking the surroundings.

"He is readying his army, I am afraid," said the Green Knight. "We must get you all to Camelot." The Green Knight lifted Bors easily.

"It is the end," said the Green Man.

When the company reached Camelot, Erec and Hector rushed to inform King Arthur. Mel and Magdalena took Bors to a bedchamber so he could rest. Bors had other plans.

"Rest?! We are under siege! I must avenge my poor, sturdy, trustworthy leg!" grumbled Bors, sitting up. The magical leaf had been extremely effective. His wound had already healed completely. "Mel, go and fetch the Green Knight for me, if you please."

Mel sighed. Bors's stubbornness had only increased with injury. She squeezed his hand and then left the room in search of the Green Knight.

Magdalena rose and also walked to the door.

"We are not in Faerie now, so I intend to use every sword I can find. I must go and prepare," she said.

"Of course," said Bors. And then, before she left:

"Magdalena. Could I have a word first? There is something . . . something I want to ask you about."

Erec and Hector stood before King Arthur and Queen Guinevere. The Round Table was filled with the greatest knights of Camelot.

Arthur took a breath.

"Very well. Let them come," said Arthur.

He stood and addressed the hall.

"Today, my good knights, we stand with the Band of the Terrible Lizards. We shall fight not only for Camelot, but for the world as we know it."

All of the knights rose from the Round Table.

"Our swords are ready," said Lancelot. He bowed. Then Lancelot turned to Erec.

"Sir Erec, you have knowledge we do not possess. Advise us, please. What do you suggest?"

Erec stood a little straighter and nodded.

"Huzzah!" roared the Round Table.

✧ ✧ ✧

The edge of the forest below Camelot shuddered. The ground rumbled. Thick vines of purple and red burst from the soil and wrapped up around the trees.

"They are coming," called Arthur from the high rampart of the castle. "Lower the drawbridge. We shall meet them on the road."

At Erec's suggestion, Arthur and all of the knights were in their finest clothing, their brightest armor. Every weapon of steel and iron was polished and ready. Ash prized glamour and style. He would be met by Camelot at its grandest.

King Arthur led the procession, followed by Erec, Magdalena, Hector, and Mel. Lancelot and Galahad, Tristan and Lamorack, Gawain and his Orkney brothers Agravaine and Gareth fell into rank, ready to fight. The Green Knight was there, too, standing beside his magnificent green horse. Bors sat on the saddle.

"Thank you again for the loan of your fine horse, Froggy," said Bors.

"I would only do so for the bravest of knights. He will serve you well, Sir Bors."

A procession approached from the forest. King Ash rode a great white stag in front. Morgause and Morgan Le Fay walked behind him. Mordred followed, riding a black horse. Behind them, thousands of creatures of every description marched. As the procession approached, more vines broke from the ground in their wake. Finally, from the deepest part of the forest, the dragon burst into the air.

"Oh my," said Galahad.

Erec turned to him.

"It's just a dragon, Galahad. Buck up."

Arthur raised his hand and the knights of Camelot rode slowly down the hill to meet the Good Folk. Aside from the horses and clanking armor, the air was still and quiet.

The two armies—the faerie army vast and terrifying, Arthur's army woefully outnumbered—met and stopped. A hundred yards separated them.

"Hello, Arthur King!" shouted Ash with a bright smile. "Surrendering?"

"No, King Ash. Not surrendering," answered Arthur.

"Hmm!" said Ash. He twisted on the stag and glanced

back at his massive army. "Are you sure?"

"Might I have a word, King Ash of Faerie?" It was the Green Knight, his voice sonorous and clear. "If that pleases you as well, Arthur."

Arthur nodded. Ash clicked his tongue.

"Be brief, Green Man," said Ash.

"Certainly. Just to be clear: you mean to spread the realm of faerie throughout Camelot, visible completely at all times?" asked the Green Knight.

"Yes," said Ash. "That is it in a nutshell."

"And you wish to wipe out the humans?"

"Oh yes. That, too. Nearly forgot," said Ash.

Morgause stirred uncomfortably and cleared her throat.

"Or maybe some will live . . . have not decided all of the details yet," said Ash with a nod to the sisters.

"Right," said the Green Knight. "But for the most part, no humans."

"Correct," said Ash.

"Once that is done, who shall we trick?" asked the Green Knight.

Ash said nothing but was clearly listening.

"Where would the fun be if we cannot spirit someone away or set up some crazy bargain that they will inevitably fall for?"

Ash opened his mouth, then closed it again in thought.

The Green Knight continued. "And if magic is everywhere, then why would we be special?"

This stung. Ash shifted on his stag.

"We need these humans for amusement and we need them as an audience, to be thrilled and spooked by our charms. After all, do Good Folk wish to be legendary . . . or commonplace?"

The Green Knight finished. Silence on both sides.

"You have a choice to make today," said King Arthur. "You *all* have a choice. Annihilation? Or Coexistence?"

A few imps and lesser faeries squeaked: "I vote coexistence!" and "Yum! Coexistence!"

After a moment Ash cleared his throat.

"Faerie retains its glory and honor?" he asked.

"Absolutely," said Arthur.

"We continue our whimsical, impish ways?"

"Of course."

"Our mystery?"

"Yes."

"Our occasional taunting of humans in their dreams?"

"I wish you wouldn't, but sure. *Occasionally*," stressed Arthur.

"These terms are to my liking. I accept," said Ash.

Morgause stormed before Ash. "No! You ridiculous creature!"

Ash snapped his

fingers. Vines burst from the ground and twisted around Morgause, binding her completely and covering her mouth.

"'Ridiculous?'" said Ash quietly. The vines tightened around Morgause. "For that outburst, I believe you will come with me, Morgause. You will reside in Faerie with your son's nightmarish friends for a time. They will enjoy that. You will not."

Arthur rode slowly up to Ash. He looked down from his saddle. Excalibur remained in its scabbard, but its hilt gleamed in the sunlight.

"No," said Arthur.

"No what?" asked Ash.

"Morgause is free to return to her home in Orkney."

"Would you have your enemies so close to you?" said Ash.

"Morgause is not my enemy."

Ash considered Arthur for a moment. The vines tightened around Morgause.

"You are a strange king," said Ash.

"I had a strange tutor."

Mel smiled.

Ash snapped again and the vines dropped to the ground. Morgause gasped for breath. She looked up at Arthur. Morgan Le Fay went to her side.

"Let us go home, sister."

Morgause nodded.

Arthur turned to Mordred. "I have no feud with you, either, Mordred. You are free to stay here or return to Orkney."

Mordred glared at Arthur and Morgause. He spat on the ground, then rode off on his horse.

Ash turned his stag, and the army of Faerie marched back toward the forest.

The procession halted. Ash looked back and called in a gleeful, loud, clear voice: "This was fun. However, I *was* looking forward to a *wee* bit of chaos. So you may keep the dragon."

And with that the dragon soared to the castle, breathing fire. The knights scattered. The dragon crashed onto a tower and began to smash Camelot to pieces.

CHAPTER FIFTEEN

D VS. D

It was astonishing how much damage a dragon could do to a castle in a short amount of time. Banners and flags in flames. The east tower demolished. A great hole in the north side of the castle wall. This last move allowed the dragon to actually enter the castle itself, which is when the real trouble began.

The Knights of the Round Table were at a loss. They did not know where or how to start. They tried lances and arrows and swords but were repeatedly

knocked back by the ferocity of the dragon.

Erec told Lancelot to take some of the knights and get all of the servants and minstrels and regular citizens out of the castle and to safety. Soon the crumbling castle was mostly deserted except for the Band of the Terrible Lizards, the Green Knight, and King Arthur.

"Sir Erec," said Mel suddenly. "I have an idea!"

"I was waiting for that," said Erec as the dragon smashed the Round Table to bits.

"King Arthur, I need something from you," said Mel quickly.

Seconds later Mel was racing up the stairs to Merlin's tower. All of Merlin's lessons, his encouragement, his kindness, his belief in her flooded through as she entered the library.

She crossed the room to the lectern. "All you really need is experience . . . ," she said, grabbing the ragged volume titled *The Terrible Lizards*.

Mel raced back through the castle.

". . . a bit of imagination . . . ," she breathed.

She skidded around a corner. Sounds of the destruction

and the dragon's screeches echoed around her.

She bolted across a great courtyard to an enormous hall in the center of Camelot. Arthur and the others were hurrying to meet her.

". . . and a problem to sink your teeth into . . ."

Arthur tossed something into the air, and Mel caught it. The tooth of the *Tyrannosaurus rex*, king of the terrible lizards. Mel placed the tooth on the floor, then arranged the book a few yards away.

Mel took a deep breath, let it out, then opened the book to a very specific page. She backed away quickly to join the others.

The torches in the hall extinguished. The evening sun shone through the small windows, but most of the hall was in shadow, including the place where the book lay.

There was a low grumble.

Magdalena had her sword ready.

From the shadows the enormous, ferocious, most terrible lizard of all stomped slowly toward the tooth. It saw the company and roared.

And then it was blindsided by the dragon. This did not sit well with the T-rex. Its powerful legs kicked the dragon off. It regained its footing and swished its thick tail. Dragon and T-rex pounced at the same time, and the hall shook with titanic chaos, thunderous blows, massive teeth, and complete destruction.

King Arthur, Mel, and the knights took cover.

"Brilliant!" said Erec.

"Um . . . just one question, though," said Hector. "How do we—uh—how does this end, exactly?"

It was a fair question. Equally matched, the T-rex had distracted the dragon and kept it safely busy (more or less), but the eventual victor in either case would be a problem.

"The lizard wants its tooth back," said Magdalena. "I took it. I'll return it."

"Yes," said Mel. "And the dragon and the terrible lizard must both become . . ." Her eyes landed on the book.

"Legends," she finished.

Mel looked up at Magdalena. "After you."

Mel and Magdalena tore into the battle, dodging claws

and tails and streams of fire. Magdalena scooped up the tooth just as Mel retrieved the enchanted book. At the same moment, they each hurled the objects.

The tooth went straight down the T-rex's throat. The book was snatched and gobbled by the dragon. Each creature paused for a moment, then the terrible lizard sunk its teeth into the back of the dragon as the dragon whipped its neck around and sunk *its* teeth into the back of the T-rex.

The hall was cast into sudden, complete darkness and eerie silence. When the torches flickered back to life, both creatures were gone.

"I think that dragon will be very much at home in the land of terrible lizards," observed Erec.

"And one day someone will discover a unique skeleton, I should imagine," said Hector.

Arthur placed a hand on Mel's shoulder.

"Well done. Well done indeed."

CHAPTER SIXTEEN

ONCE & FUTURE

The sun was about to rise. Camelot—or the castle, to be more accurate—was in ruins. King Arthur, Mel, Erec, Magdalena, Hector, and Bors sat on a hillside overlooking the wreckage.

"It was a good castle," said Arthur. "We will rebuild it."

"Do you think Morgause will return?" asked Erec.

"I do not think so," said Arthur. "Morgan Le Fay—although not entirely trustworthy—is mostly peaceful. She can be very persuasive, and I believe Morgause

will ultimately agree with her."

"Mordred is still out there," said Mel, staring at the spot she last saw the strange, angry boy.

"True," said Arthur. "We shall meet again in time. But not today, Mel. Not today."

The sky brightened from an indigo to a soft pink and orange hue.

Hector was staring at one particular section of the castle.

"At least Merlin's tower has survived, along with his books, thank goodness."

"Yes," said Arthur. "That reminds me, good Sir Hector. I would hate for all of Merlin's collected volumes to be neglected, gather dust, and—much worse—be unread. Would you consider the possibility of being a caretaker for the library?"

Hector gulped.

"Sire."

"I understand if you'd rather not. It would require a great deal of 'inside work' and give you less time for adventuring and so forth," said Arthur.

"I . . . I think I could muster that," said Hector, bubbling with excitement.

"Excellent. Thank you," said Arthur.

"Well," began Bors. "I suppose my adventuring will also be curtailed a bit now. But no long faces! I have a plan!"

"Do tell," said Erec.

"I have consulted with my good comrade Magdalena, who knows of such things, and I have decided to become a blacksmith."

"Oh!" said Hector pleasantly.

"Yes!" said Bors with a thrill in his voice. "Smithing. The clang of the hammer on molten iron, sparks flying everywhere, smoke and steam and honest dirt under my nails. And the first thing that I shall make will be . . ." He paused dramatically. "A mighty sword leg!"

"Sword leg?" asked Erec.

"Yes! A sword where my leg once was, you see!"

"But Bors, dear fellow," said Hector kindly, "with each

step you took you would sink into the ground. You would always be stuck somewhere."

Bors considered this.

"Ah. That is true. You were always the smart one, my friend. Fine. *Mace* leg, it is!"

Erec laughed, looking down at the new spring grass.

"And what of you, Sir Erec? What will you do without my constant company?" asked Bors.

"Oh, I don't know. . . ." Erec trailed off. He stared into the distance. "I might . . . there is a fair maiden . . . no, that's not quite right. Bit of a spitfire, actually. Back on Orkney. Greer is her name."

"You wish to court her, Erec?" said Magdalena with a smile.

"Not exactly *court* her. I don't know how that would go. I don't know if she even likes me. I just want to talk with her again. Not sure why, but there it is," he finished.

"Perhaps you'll settle down in Orkney," said Bors.

"Maybe not *Orkney*," said Erec. "I hear Ireland is nice, though."

"Magdalena?" asked Arthur. "What say you, Black Knight?"

"I am a knight, my king. I will fight by your side as long as knights are needed."

"Good to hear," said Arthur.

Magdalena turned now to Mel, who sat beside her.

"And you, Melancholy Postlethwaite," she said. "You have been a squire, an archer, and a budding magician. What does the future hold for you?"

Mel thought for a moment, watching the sun rise. She smiled.

"I think there is still more in the world for me to discover, Magdalena. I truly do not yet know what I will be."

"I am sure it will be extraordinary," said Magdalena. She hugged Mel close.

They all sat in contented silence for a while, listening to the chirping of the birds.

Eventually Erec cleared his throat.

"Sire, have I ever told you about the time I slew forty dragons?"

"I do not believe you told the whole story, Sir Erec," said Arthur.

Erec lay back with his hands behind his head.

"Well then, settle in. It is quite a splendid tale indeed. . . ."

A NOTE
FROM
THE BRIDGE TROLL

I have been around a long time. By "around" I mean under my bridge, but that bridge has been crossed by all of the greats and not-so-greats at one time or another.

Now, I try to have an open mind about people. I am still waiting for my goats from that last band of knights, but they still might come through, so I will reserve judgment for the moment. However, here are some of my thoughts on some other big names of our Age, along with a helpful ranking of my own devising.

King Arthur

Where does one start? Did you know that he became king when he was still a boy because he pulled a sword from a stone? I am not even kidding. Speaking of swords, Excalibur (you know a sword is good when it has a name) was given to Arthur by *the* Lady of the Lake. None of that has gone to his head, though. Arthur is a good man through and through, the tops of your species, in my humble opinion. A great and wise ruler, a kind and thoughtful gentleman in an age of brutes, and a regular Joe who always has time for a chat with an old troll. The legends of Arthur are many and well worth reading.

Rating: FIVE GOATS

Sir Lancelot

His full name is Lancelot of the Lake, or "du Lac" if you are being fancy. That is because he was raised by the Lady of the Lake. Wonder why she never gave *him* Excalibur? He seems worthy, with many adventures and heroic deeds to his credit. Everyone will tell you that Lancelot is the greatest of the Knights of the Round Table. Everyone but Lancelot, that is. He is a troubled one in some respects. Dwells on his own character flaws. I am no gossip, but there have been whispers about Lancelot and . . . No! I shan't spread rumors. Look him up yourself if you are curious.

Rating: FOUR GOATS

Morgan Le Fay

Morgan gets a bad name in some of the stories. Personally, I've always liked her. She has a wicked sense of humor. Unfortunately, she can also be just plain wicked. We all have our bad days! You will find Morgan Le Fay in many tales about Arthur and Merlin. They are all different enough from one another to make you wonder: Who is the *real* Morgan Le Fay?

Rating: FOUR GOATS

Sir Galahad

Another of the great ones, although just between you and me, his good looks and general air of perfection are a bit much at times. Some say he is actually the son of Lancelot, which would explain his knightly valor but, again, I am not going to peddle hearsay. His legends will explain the whole story, including the fact that he eventually found that Grail everyone wanted.

Rating: THREE AND A HALF GOATS

Sir Lamorack

Ugh. *That* guy.

Rating: ONE GOAT

You want more? You're not even offering me a chicken, let alone a goat! No, I am tired. It is nap time under the bridge. If you want to know more about Arthur, Merlin, and the Knights of the Round Table, you can find ample stories of their adventures. Happy reading.

Now go away.

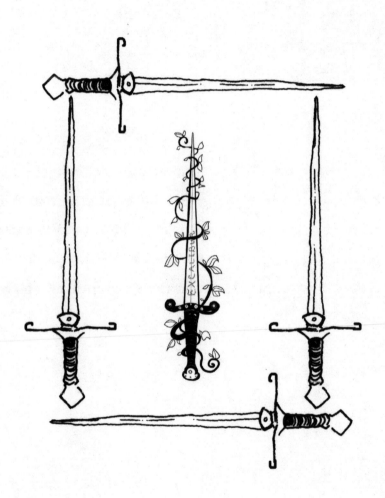

A NOTE FROM THE AUTHOR

I fell in love with King Arthur and his knights as a kid, mostly through books. Today, you can find several excellent versions, some that tell the tales faithfully and some that (ahem) stretch the premise a bit. Here is a list of the books that sparked my interest years ago and remain personal favorites to this day.

—*Matt Phelan*

The Story of King Arthur and His Knights, written and illustrated by Howard Pyle

The Story of the Champions of the Round Table, written and illustrated by Howard Pyle

King Arthur, adapted by Sidney Lanier and illustrated by N. C. Wyeth

Tales of King Arthur, written by James Riordan and illustrated by Victor Ambrus

Prince Valiant in the Court of King Arthur, written and illustrated by Hal Foster

Castles by Alan Lee, written by David Day

The Once and Future King, written by T. H. White

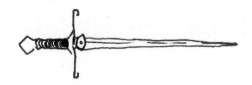

MATT PHELAN is the author and illustrator of many books for young readers. The first book in this series, *Knights vs. Dinosaurs*, was named an ALA Notable Book and an Indie Next Pick, as well nominated for several state awards. His graphic novels include the *New York Times*-bestselling *Snow White*, which was named a best book of the year by *Publishers Weekly*, *Wall Street Journal*, *School Library Journal*, and the New York Public Library; *Storm in the Barn*, winner of the Scott O'Dell Award; *Around the World*; and *Bluffton*. He is also the author and illustrator of the picture books *Pignic* and *Druthers*, and has illustrated several books by other authors, including *The Higher Power of Lucky*, by Susan Patron, winner of the Newbery Medal. Matt Phelan lives with his family in Pennsylvania.